THE LAND BEFORE TIME
COLLECTION

D1507428

Let's Play impossible

by
Hildy Mesnik & Barbara Slate

"Whe-e-e! This is fun!" squealed Ducky on this happy day
in The Great Valley.

"Great slide!" said Littlefoot as he held the tree in place for
his friend. Spike was pleased that he could help and snack at
the same time.

"Me, next!" called out Petrie, the only flyer of the five pals.
SPLAS-S-SH!

"Hey! Watch where you're sliding!" scolded Cera.
She had been snoozing in the sun just a moment ago.
   "Oh, I am sorry. Yes, I am," apologized Ducky.
   Littlefoot stifled a grin, "Why don't you take a turn, Cera?"
   "I might as well," grumbled the unhappy three-horn.
"Since I'm all wet anyway!"

CRA-A-ACK!

"Oh, no!" cried Littlefoot, watching the tree break apart under his friend.

"Yep, yep, yep," said Ducky, the cheerful swimmer. "Cera slipped on the slide!"

"Me can't look," fretted Petrie. Spike buried his head in the sand so he wouldn't have to see.

"Oww!" yelled Cera, crashing into the water. "I don't like this game!"

The enormous splash almost knocked over Petrie. "Hey! Petrie have birdbath yesterday."

"This isn't any fun," said Cera, trying to hide her embarrassment. "I want to play something else!"

"How about leap frog?" suggested Ducky.

"Borrr-ing," sniffed Cera, sticking her nose in the air.

"Do you want to play hide-and-seek?" asked Littlefoot.

Cera answered with a l-o-n-g yawn. " I want to do something I've never done before," she said. "Something impossible!"

"But doing the impossible," said a puzzled Ducky, "is impossible!"

Cera gripped the slippery log. "You hatchlings just watch what I can do!"

"Wait for us, Cera," called Ducky. "We want to have fun, too."

Cera stood up on the log and bragged, "Look at me!"

The friends were amazed! "That's a good trick, Cera," said Ducky.

Petrie flapped his wings and applauded. "Cera do the impossible," he crowed. "Cera dance on water!"

Even Spike stopped eating to marvel at the silly sight. But Littlefoot wasn't laughing.

Suddenly the log began to pitch beneath Cera's feet.
Slip-slide-splash . . . Cera spilled into the water!
   "Hurry, everyone!" shouted Littlefoot. "Cera needs help!"
The friends rushed over to the spot where she had sunk.
   "I will save you, Cera!" said Ducky. The brave swimmer
plunged into the water.

Under the water, Cera was falling right towards a giant clam. "Oof!" she said, landing right on poor Mr. Clam and waking him up.

"Hey!" cried out Mr. Clam. "I said not to wake me up until supper. Can't a clam get any sleep around here?"

Cera tried to apologize, but only bubbles came out.

"P-tooey!" said Mr. Clam, spitting out the unexpected visitor. "Either that was a confused three-horn taking a dip or the fattest blowfish I ever saw."

WHO-O-O-SH! Cera spurted up through the water.

"Just get me back to my friends," she thought, "and I promise I'll never show off again!"

"I saw her land right over here" said Petrie, landing on a mound of mud.

"Get off me, beak brain!" scowled the muddy lump.

"It's Cera! She's okay," said Ducky, happily. Spike licked Cera's face clean with joy.

"Ha! Escaping from that mean old giant clam was nothing," scoffed Cera, already forgetting her promise. "I want to do something impossible!"

"How about finding our way home?" asked Ducky.

"It's that way!" blurted Cera and Littlefoot at the same time, but pointing in different directions. Spike decided the right direction for him was toward the juicy green shoot at his feet.

Petrie noticed his own tummy beginning to rumble. "Petrie hungry. But which way is dinner?"

Littlefoot had an idea. "Look up in the sky. The twinklys will guide us home!"

Cera brightened. "You scaredy eggs go home to your nice warm dinners. I'm going to catch a twinkly."

"But, Cera," said Littlefoot, "Even my grandpa, who has the longest neck in The Great Valley, couldn't possibly reach a twinkly."

"Hmph! I'll have a twinkly if it's the last thing I – Yikes!" Cera slipped and took a wild tumble!

"Ugh," said Cera as she crashed into a giant spider web.
    "It may just be the last thing she does," said Ducky.
"I hope those spiders have had their dinners!"
    But the blow bounced Cera right out of the web.
Down she tumbled into the darkness.
    "We're coming, Cera!" yelled her friends as they ran
to catch her.

Littlefoot reached out and caught his falling friend just in time. "Gotcha!" he said, holding fast to Cera's tail.

"Mmph mmph," said Petrie, gripping Cera's frill with his beak.

Suddenly Cera noticed something bright and sparkling right in front of her nose!

"A twinkly! I touched it!" she cried as her nose brushed a glowing firefly. "I did the impossible!"

A puzzled Petrie let loose Cera's frill. "Twinkly is flier?" he asked.

But Littlefoot couldn't hold Cera much longer and she clattered to the ground in a heap!

"Ooh," moaned Cera. "Impossible is one thing—a horn-ache is another."

"Can we possibly go home now?" asked Ducky.

The next day, the bright circle shone high in the sky.
The friends were happy, safe, and well-fed.

"Whe-e-e! This is fun!" whooped Cera.

Littlefoot grinned as he watched his friend slide merrily down
Grandpa's neck. "Good slide, Cera," he said. "Sometimes doing
the same old thing is more fun than you can possibly imagine!"